# ANTARCTIC Ice Flight

My sincere thanks to the following organisation for their time, information, images and enthusiasm for this book:

The Australian Antarctic Division, a division of the Australian Department of the Environment, Water, Heritage and the Arts.

Dear Reader

I love getting on a plane and flying to different countries and places. It's always exciting stepping on board, buckling your seat belt, taking off, and looking out the window at the ground far below.

> **THE ANTARCTIC ICE FLIGHT IS WAITING FOR DEPARTURE!**

Imagine how exciting it would be to get on a flight to the world's coldest, windiest, and driest continent! The lucky scientists, engineers and support crews who travel to the Antarctic to work and study have a really exciting flight to look forward to.

Are you ready to join us? The Antarctic ice flight is waiting to depart!

John Parsons

NELSON
CENGAGE Learning™
For learning solutions, visit cengage.com.au

Contents

# ANTARCTIC Ice Flight

# 1 Fly to the Coldest Place

## No **Ordinary** Flight

icebergs break away from Antarctica

In two weeks we'll catch a plane. But this flight is no ordinary flight. You can't just buy a ticket, pack your suitcase, and turn up to the airport. There are no tourists on this flight, only people like scientists who will be working in Antarctica.

### The Coldest Continent

This is a flight to the Antarctic, the coldest continent in the world. It is an environment that must be treated with a lot of care and respect.

### Planning for the Flight

We need to start training and planning for our flight from Hobart, Tasmania, to the Antarctic. We begin many days ahead of our trip.

## The Antarctic Landscape

Antarctica is the driest, windiest and coldest continent in the world. The Antarctic continent is a landmass covered with ice, some of it up to four kilometres thick. There is also some exposed rock. Millions of years ago Antarctica was heavily vegetated, but now the only plants left are mosses and lichens.

*an Airbus A319-115LR*

# 2 Packed for the Ice Flight

TEXT TYPE
Recount

## Six **Steps** to **Prepare**

In December last year, we were planning to visit Antarctica. We needed to catch a plane from Tasmania, Australia. Our flight would be one of about 20 flights that this plane makes to the Antarctic each year. Our plane would carry 20 passengers. In emergencies, it's also used as a flying ambulance.

Before leaving, we had to do some training and learn more about how to prepare for our trip.

### Step 1

Well before our flight, everyone attended training in Tasmania, Australia. This helped us prepare for the trip to Antarctica.

### Step 2

One thing we were told was that we could take only 45 kilograms of baggage each. That sounded like quite a lot, but there are no shops in Antarctica.

*training in Tasmania*

### Step 3

On our first day of training, we caught a special bus to Kingston in Tasmania, where we had a busy day of learning about the trip.

## Step 4

We were measured, weighed and given health checks. We were also given the clothing and things that we needed to live and work in the freezing cold Antarctic conditions.

## Step 5

We were told that most of the special clothing had to be returned when we got back to Australia, for the next group of travellers.

But it was good to know that some items – like our thermal underwear – were not recycled. We could keep those!

## Step 6

We couldn't use any of our special clothing before we got on the plane. Antarctica is a protected environment, so we had to keep our clothes clean so that seeds and insects couldn't hitch a ride.

We were also warned that if we wanted to take any of our own clothing, it had to be washed in bleach.

We had to be extra careful about shoes, which could carry hidden pests or dirt on the soles.

*getting our Antarctic clothing*

*packing our Antarctic clothing*

After the training, we knew what clothes we would need and what to pack. We were now ready to learn more about the trip.

# 3 Learn About the Plane

## **Airbus** A319-115LR

When we fly to the Antarctic, we will catch an Airbus A319-115LR. This plane can fly 5000 nautical miles on one load of fuel.

> **NAUTICAL MILES**
>
> 1 nautical mile = 1.852 km, so 5000 nautical miles = 9260 km
>
> **km (kilometre)**

### Enough Fuel

The plane can fly the 4000 kilometres from Hobart to Antarctica and back without refuelling. This is useful, because fuel doesn't need to be stored in Antarctica. It can be dangerous and could pollute Antarctica.

It also means that if something goes wrong, or we can't land in Antarctica, we will have enough fuel to get home safely.

*the icy runway awaits the Airbus*

Airbus A319-115LR

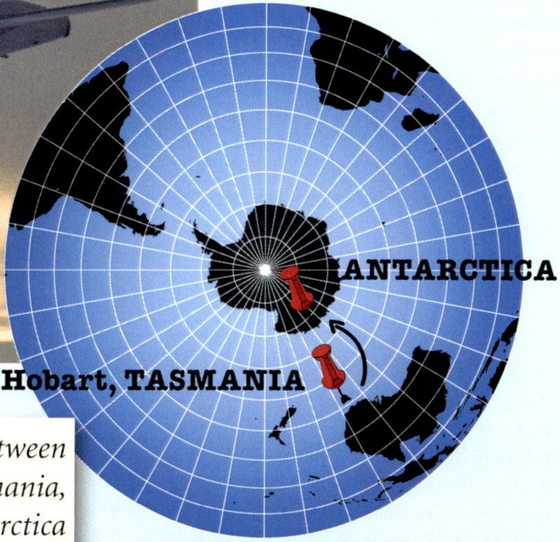

ANTARCTICA

Hobart, TASMANIA

The Airbus flies between Hobart, Tasmania, and Antarctica

History

## Aircraft Expeditions in Antarctica

In 1911, Sir Douglas Mawson wanted to use an early plane during his explorations in Commonwealth Bay, Antarctica. But the plane had an accident before it left Australia, so it was never used.

Australian adventurer Sir Hubert Wilkins was the first to fly over the Antarctic continent on 16 November 1928. The aerodrome used for Antarctic flights is named after him.

Sir Douglas Mawson

Australian expeditions have used aircraft in Antarctica for over 70 years.

# 4 Planning the Route

## Flight to the Wilkins Aerodrome

We plan to fly to Wilkins Aerodrome, which is 70 kilometres south-east of the Australian base at Casey. The route will take us over the sea, thick ice shelves and the continent of Antarctica.

### WILKINS AERODROME

The Wilkins Aerodrome was named after Sir George Hubert Wilkins who was an Australian flyer and polar explorer.

### What Is the Runway Built On?

Because the runway is built on ice, it moves south at around 12 metres every year. It's important that the pilots have accurate navigation maps.

We don't want to use last year's maps!

## Where Is the Aerodrome Built?

The Wilkins Aerodrome is about 700 metres above sea level, where the average temperature is about -14° C. It was built on a high spot so it would stay frozen. If it was built any lower, during summer the runway could melt.

## When Can Planes Fly to Antarctica?

Planes can only fly to Antarctica during the summer months which are from November to February in the Southern Hemisphere.

During the winter, it is too dark and the weather is too dangerous for planes to fly and land on the ice.

Technology

### How to Flatten an Ice Runway

*The hard ice on the top of the runway is made flat using a laser-guided grader fitted with a huge ice-cutting blade.*

**TEMPERATURE**

In 1983, the lowest temperature recorded was -89.2° C at Vostok, which is in the Australian Antarctic Territory.

*an Adélie penguin in Antarctica*

**HISTORY FEATURE**

# A Wilkins Runway Time Line

For many years people dreamed of flying from Australia to the Antarctic. It would be faster for scientists and supplies to go by air than by ship.

An aerodrome with a runway had to be built.

visibility is low over the Wilkins runway

## 1996

Work began on the Wilkins runway. First, the Australian Government asked experts for advice before building started.

- Where should the runway go?
- How could it be built on ice?
- What types of aircraft could fly there and back without refuelling?
- Which aircraft were safest?
- What rules were needed to protect the Antarctic from harm?

## 2002

The government began building a small test runway.

## 2003

The government finished the small test runway.

"What are they building over there?"

"Is this where we check in?"

## 2004

Two small planes fitted with skis landed safely on the small test runway. The test was a success.

## 2005

Work began on the large runway. Many different aircraft were tested to see which was best.

## 2006

The Airbus was chosen to fly to and from the Antarctic.

## 2007

The large runway was finished. It was tested when the first Airbus landed successfully. All the navigation systems worked, too.

## 2008

The airport was opened for the first official flight.

the runway in action

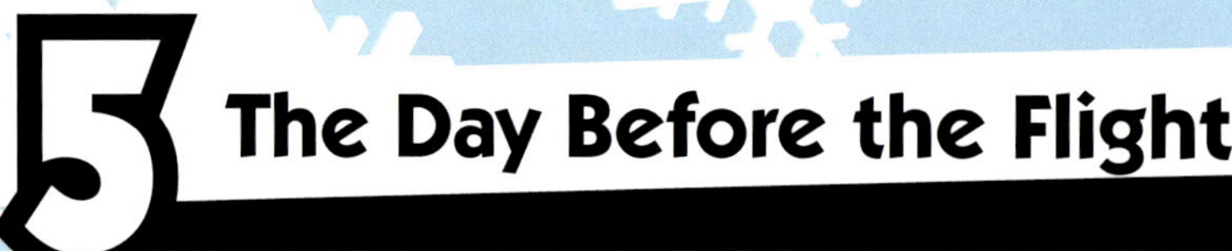

# 5 The Day Before the Flight

## The **Final** Meeting

Everyone has to attend a meeting on the day before we leave. Our flight coordinator tells us how to prepare for our flight.

### Wait for a Text Message

The weather in Antarctica is unpredictable. We have to wait until 5.00 pm for our flight to be confirmed.

Then everyone gets a text message telling us whether the flight will go or not!

*a fine day to land at the icy Antarctic aerodrome*

## Air Service to Antarctica

US Antarctic Air Base

Many countries have aerodromes in Antarctica. The biggest air service to Antarctica flies out of Christchurch, New Zealand. Here, the United States National Guard and the Royal New Zealand Airforce fly huge Hercules, C17 Globemaster or Airbus aircraft to McMurdo Sound in the Antarctic.

Flights from Christchurch can take up to seven hours. If you're unlucky enough to be flying on a Hercules, you sit on webbing seats in the cargo compartment. In the information that passengers are given before the flight, everyone is told to "bring their sense of humour".

# 6 The Day of the Flight

## An **Early** Start

We are told that our departure time from Hobart can change. The weather in Antarctica may get worse.

The best time to land at Wilkins Aerodrome is early in the morning. We know that we have to be ready to leave Hobart any time between midnight and 5.00 am.

### At the Airport

It's an early start. Like all international flights, we have to be at the airport in plenty of time to check-in and go through Customs.

Everyone has to show their a passport – even going to Antarctica – because we are leaving the country.

**CUSTOMS**

Customs is a government department that protects a country from unwanted diseases, plant pests, animal pests, stolen wildlife and other illegal things. It prevents people from bringing them into or sending them out of the country.

loading luggage

Social Studies

## What NOT to Take!

*Run away! Here comes another plane!*

It is very important not to take plant material, including seeds, fruit and vegetables, fauna and soil, to Antarctica. These could have disastrous effects on the Antarctic wildlife and environment.

Plastic packaging can kill birds if adult birds mistake it for food and give it to their chicks. Poultry and egg products can also transmit diseases to penguins and other birds.

# 7 The Flight

## Our **Flight** to **Antarctica**

"What's for breakfast?"

Our flight to Antarctica will take about four-and-a-half hours. The excitement builds throughout the flight.

Some people read. Some talk. Others work. Everyone feels like they are part of a special team.

### Our Survival Clothes

Shortly before we descend, we are told to change into our survival clothes.

Now it is getting really exciting.

Everyone unpacks their bright red kit bag and gets dressed in their polar gear.

We are told that we must wear our survival clothes for the rest of the trip, until we reach our base safely.

"Get ready to descend."

## The Plane Descends

The plane starts to descend. We spot the airfield. While we have been flying, the one-and-a-half kilometres of icy runway has been carefully cleared of snow, checked and re-checked to make sure it is safe to land.

We fasten our seatbelts, and look at the continent that will be our home for the next few weeks.

## Welcome to Antarctica!

Touchdown!

# 8 Landing on Ice

## A Cloud of **Snow** and **Ice**

With a roar of its engines, and in a cloud of snow and ice, our plane lands. Everyone in the cabin cheers and claps.

Our flight to the Antarctic was special. It was more exciting than any other plane trips.

The Airbus will spend around two hours on the Wilkins runway before it is ready to fly back to Tasmania.

### Our Work Begins

We are all eager to leave the plane and get started. Everyone has a different job to do for the next two weeks.

We will enjoy studying this special continent.

Before we know it, it will be time for another ice flight – this time, heading back home!

Social Studies

## Seven Countries Work Together

There are no cities or states in the Antarctic. The only places where people live are bases or stations. Seven countries claim territory in Antarctica, and all of them have agreed to cooperate with other countries to study and protect Antarctica for the benefit of the world.

The Airbus lands on the runway.

## GEOGRAPHY FEATURE

# Discover Antarctica's Map

breaking up the ice

an Antarctic sealion

## The Size of Antarctica

Including all of its islands and ice shelves, Antarctica is nearly twice the size of Australia. It covers 13 661 000 square kilometres.

*expedition ship in Antarctic waters*

*a runway grader*

*King penguins*

# Index



# Glossary

| | |
|---|---|
| continent | One of seven large landmasses: North America, South America, Africa, Asia, Australia, Antarctica or Europe |
| fauna | The group of animals that can be found in an area |
| landmass | An area of land (usually large) |
| lichens | Organisms that are a mixture of a fungus and a bacteria, or a fungus and a simple plant |
| mosses | Small, simple plants that grow in shady areas and do not have flowers or seeds |
| thermal | A type of clothing that is designed to keep the wearer warm in cold conditions |
| vegetated | Covered with living plants |
| webbing | Straps of material, woven together in a criss-cross pattern for strength |